# Hotel Inspection

# Hotel Inspection

ANNIKA STOUT

Annika Stout
ORCA - Calle Gil-Vernet 54/55
Les Tapies 1 #1087
Hospitalet de l'Infant, Tarragona 43890
Spain
https://annikastout.com

# Contents

*For all of you naughty girls who pretend to be innocent but secretly like getting spanked and fu**ed hard.*

*Don't worry….I'll keep your secret!*

**P**rime *parking. It's my lucky day,* she thought.

Kimberly threw her sneakers, socks, and dress in the trunk of her little red car, then took the soccer ball and a bottle of water and ran over to the beach. Alicia was already waiting for her, doing stretches on a towel.

The beach was almost empty today, quite the contrast to the crowds that came to town on the weekends, looking like a bunch of ants in the sand.

It had its advantages to work most weekends and then have days off during the week when everyone else was at work.

Alicia waved when she spotted Kimberly. They have been best friends ever since they both joined the all-girls soccer team when they were only five years old.

"Eye candy on the left?" Kimberly asked Alicia, wondering if she'd noticed as well.

He was the only guy on the beach, sitting in a beach chair reading. Kimberly had a weak spot for the nerdy guys. There was nothing sexier than a man reading a book.

Alicia jumped to her feet and grabbed the ball from Kimberly.

"Time to find out!"

She kicked the ball up in the air and then passed it on to Kimberly with precision. More than 20 years of playing soccer together had taught them enough to impress any kind of man. While passing the ball between each other and showing off their best tricks, they moved slowly towards him.

"Is he looking at all?" Alicia asked.

"Nope. This is a tough cookie. I think he is wearing glasses, maybe he can't see that far. Let's try for a close call."

Alicia took the hint and shot the ball with force in his direction. It dropped down merely ten feet away from him. She ran after the ball while Kimberly kept an eye on the guy.

*What's wrong with him?* He didn't even look up.

Alicia came back running, kicking the ball in front of her.

"Definitely eye candy. Muscular but not too

muscular and yes he has glasses. You should check him out yourself, he's *totally* your type, Kim."

Alicia was amazing, while being happy in her own relationship, she was always up for finding a man for her best friend.

"Ok, I'll take the next one but watch him if he looks. He didn't look up at all before."

To not be too obvious, they continued playing pass for a bit before Kimberly shot the ball over to her mystery man. She decided to kick the ball to his other side this time, ruling out that the sun blocked his view, blinding him.

Kimberly ran after the ball. Her hook was in the water. All she needed now was for the fish to bite.

She slowed down when she got closer, taking her time to check out the guy in the beach chair.

*Wow!* He *absolutely* was her type. He was hot enough to be anyone's type. If he could only look up from his book now. Why wasn't he looking?

It was time to use her secret weapon. Her number one asset.

In slow motion Kimberly bent over, presenting her tanned soccer butt in a sports bikini to the mystery man. Then she jogged back, concentrating on perfect posture just in case he was looking after her.

"He's not looking, Kimberly, but you do look hot!" Alicia was giggling.

"Do you think he's gay? He is *fucking* hot, that would be *such* a waste of a man!"

Alicia flipped the ball up in the air with her foot, dribbling it from knee to knee.

"Well Kimberly, that's up to you to find out. You can always go for the *accidental* shot. Just please don't break his glasses, they look so sexy and serious on him, that would be a real shame."

They both burst out in laughter and Kimberly almost missed Alicia passing the ball over to her.

Kimberly aimed precisely and then kicked the ball. She started running immediately after it.

*Bingo*, she thought.

The soccer ball hit the guy right on the chest, making him drop his book in surprise.

"Sorry, I'm *so* sorry," she called from afar.

The man got up from his beach chair. He bent down and picked up the ball. Kimberly was positively surprised to see that he was more than a head taller than her. She wasn't exactly short herself and taller men were hard to find.

"Are you okay? I'm really so sorry about that!"

She put on her most innocent smile while holding her hands out to take the ball.

The man took a step back, eyeing Kimberly through his black horn-rimmed glasses. He did not seem happy. Not happy at all. His big hands were wrapped around her soccer ball.

"Some people on this beach wish to relax." His voice had that sexy lecturing tone in it. "Luckily the beach is almost empty today. Kicking your stupid ball around a few hundred feet west would not have bothered anyone. Please do everyone a favor and either stay on the soccer field or don't be so clumsy kicking the ball around without any skills and control."

*What? Did he just call me clumsy? No skills? Is he for real?*

Kimberly's blood began to boil. How could this good-looking nerd be so rude and arrogant? He didn't even know her. If he had bothered paying attention to them playing soccer for just a minute, he would have seen that Alicia and she had more skills and control over the ball than most men.

*How dare he belittle me like this?* Telling her she had no skills? A typical man, thinking the sport belonged to them, that women couldn't play soccer.

"If you're done lecturing me, give me my ball back!" she said.

"The only thing I'll give you is a spanking over my

knee if *you* don't turn around *immediately* and let me read my book in peace!"

He glared at Kimberly, as she tried to make sense of his threat.

*Did he really just threaten me with a spanking?* she wondered. Anger and arousal mixed together.

She held his gaze for as long as she could, which wasn't very long. The tall man, who was probably about 10 years older than her, was intimidating.

He wouldn't give in, she could see that. There was no other option than to take what she had left of her dignity and leave without the ball.

"What happened Kimberly? Where's the ball?" Alicia asked.

"He's an arrogant asshole, that's what happened. And he won't give me back my ball."

"What?" Alicia looked shocked but Kimberly laughed.

"Just wait and see, I have a surprise coming for him."

She jogged over to her car and shortly after returned with another soccer ball.

*Chapter Two*

Kimberly was proud to have gotten the position as a receptionist at the town's finest 5-star hotel but the shift work was challenging. Especially the early shift.

Making it just in time for 5:59 AM, she was shocked to see a guest waiting at the front desk counter already.

"Good morning, how can I help you Sir?" she greeted the man politely while approaching her desk.

"It's you!" he answered.

The man's voice wasn't friendly at all.

Kimberly looked up and her blood froze. The arrogant guy from the beach stood right in front of her. In her rush to make it on time, she had not recognized him. He looked different, dressed in jeans and a dress shirt, wearing shiny brown leather shoes that perfectly matched his belt. She couldn't decide which version looked hotter. Almost naked, showing off his adonis body on the beach the other day or dressed like this.

"Yes, it's me. How can I help you, Sir?"

She was proud of herself, keeping her cool and answering professionally.

"I need breakfast in my room."

"Of course, no problem. Let me get the menu for you, Sir."

Kimberly turned to get the menu but he stopped her.

"No need. I will have a coffee, black. Hot milk on the side. Two toasts, wholewheat with olive oil on it. An avocado, sliced. A hard-boiled egg, a banana, and a bottle of sparkling water. The Italian one, not the cheap brand. Make sure nothing is missing. Room 224."

He turned around and left Kimberly staring after him with her mouth open. Her heart was racing.

*What the heck was that?* she wondered. Who is this man and who eats avocados for breakfast at 6:00 AM?

Quickly she grabbed a piece of paper, scribbling down everything she remembered.

*Make sure nothing is missing? And if not? Are you going to spank me for it?*

Even if she did remember, what were the chances that the kitchen wouldn't screw up his fancy order?

Kimberly picked up the phone and called the kitchen. James answered the phone. She liked the young sous-chef. He was always in a great mood which was contagious.

"Right on time, 6:00 AM breakfast order for our VIP guest. What did he order this time, granola or avocado?"

Kimberly laughed, relieved that James was already familiar with Mr. Arrogant.

"It's avocado and I'm so glad you already know him because I'm not sure I got his order right."

"Uff, I hope for you and me that you *do* remember. Everyone knows him, Kimberly. Nicolas Charbonneau is the owner's son. He stays here every couple of weeks to make sure the hotel is running smoothly and gets one or two people fired if he's not happy. Actually, I'm pretty sure you got the position of someone getting fired the last time he came around."

Kimberly broke out in a sweat.

*Back to sending out CVs,* she thought. *I might as well quit now, to not give him the satisfaction of having me fired.*

Sure enough, Mr. Charbonneau didn't leave her waiting for long, to wonder whether or not she had remembered his posh breakfast order correctly.

At 6:55 AM the front desk phone rang. On the display an internal phone call from room 224 showed up.

Kimberly's heart was racing as she picked up.

"Front Desk, good morning. How can I help you?"

"I've ordered *hot* milk with my coffee, not *warm* milk. I've asked you to not forget *anything* about my order."

Kimberly took deep breaths to calm her anger. How was this her fault if the kitchen screwed up?

"I will make sure to instruct our kitchen staff in more detail next time. I apologize for any inconvenience Sir."

*I can do this*, she pep-talked herself. She wouldn't let him make her feel insecure or not good enough at her job. In fact, she knew she was excellent at it and she wouldn't just give up and run away because of him.

"I want you to fix it right now. I need another coffee with *hot* milk in my room *now!*"

"Of course Mr. Charbonneau, I will make sure -"

The tooting sound of the hung-up phone was all she heard.

*Wow, rude would be an understatement.*

Luckily her colleague Jessica had just arrived, allowing Kimberly to take care of her special guest.

"Sorry Jess, I'll be back in a few minutes. I have to make sure the coffee order of *Mr. Charbonneau* gets to his room burning hot."

Jessica rolled her eyes, confirming she was quite familiar with Mr. Charming as well.

---

Coffee tray in her left hand, Kimberly knocked on the door of room 224.

"Come in. Leave the coffee on my desk," Mr. Charbonneau called from inside the room.

Swiping the key card, she let herself in. The room was tidy and the windows were open, letting in a fresh breeze.

She was relieved but somehow disappointed at the same time that her special guest stayed in the bathroom. She wanted him to know that she wasn't intimidated by him.

Kimberly left the tray on the desk as instructed, next to the open laptop. Turning around to leave, Nicolas Charbonneau stepped out of the bathroom right in front of her. Her heart stopped.

Covered merely with a small towel around his

hips, the water of his wet hair was still dripping on his shoulders. Kimberly stared at his chest, which was glistening with water droplets.

Quickly she lifted her gaze but regretted it when his intense eyes locked with hers. He wasn't wearing his glasses, no protective shield between his and her eyes to soften the shock.

He obviously hadn't expected *her* to bring up the coffee, and she hadn't been mentally prepared to find him almost naked in his room.

Luckily, Kimberly recovered from the surprise first.

"Your coffee is served Mr. Charbonneau, don't burn yourself."

*1:0 for Kimberly Jones.*

The following day, Kimberly worked on late shift. It was a busy evening. Countless check-ins followed by an insane amount of questions by the guests.

Kimberly's mouth already felt fuzzy from explaining the shortest way to restaurants and local sights, highlighting them on the maps, again and again.

Since the hot coffee incident, she had not seen her *special* guest anymore but the colleagues of the early shift reassured her that he had not checked out yet. They've had their own share of adventure with him.

Apparently, the banana of his fancy breakfast order wasn't ripe enough and James had to quickly run to the closest grocery store to find a ripe banana.

Kimberly was on guard.

When the front desk phone rang, she somehow knew which number the display would show, before seeing it.

*Here we go again. You've got this.*

"Front Desk, good evening. How may I help you?"

"I have a burnt light bulb, I need someone to fix it."

"Of course Mr. Charbonneau. Which light is the broken one?"

"The main light on the ceiling," he answered.

"Thank you, Sir, someone will be with you shortly."

Kimberly paged maintenance. It didn't take long for George to call her back.

"A light bulb? Sorry, but that's not an emergency. I'm not driving back to work to exchange a light bulb."

"But it's Mr. Charbonneau, George. He'll fire me, or you, or both of us if no one fixes the light tonight."

George snorted.

"I'm not scared of him, I've known him since he was a kid and even if he'd wanted to fire me, his father would never agree. He either waits until tomorrow at 8:00 AM or you can go change it your-self if you're worried about your job. You can find the spare bulbs in the maintenance storage room on the shelf, all the way at the end on the left."

Kimberly hung up feeling slightly nauseous.

"What did he say?" asked Jessica.

"He's not coming."

Kimberly weighed out her options. She knew she had to fix it, she told him already that someone would be with him shortly.

*Call him and tell him they can only do it in the morning?* That would probably cost her her job.

"Ok, I'll do it," she said.

Light bulb in hand, she took a deep breath before knocking on the door of room 224. She was ready to get the job done. She was ready to prove to him and herself once again that there was no reason to fire her.

Nicolas Charbonneau opened the door, dressed in jeans only. The surprise to see Kimberly at his door was written all over his face before he quickly hid it.

*2:0 for Kimberly Jones,* she thought.

The room was dim. Lit up only by the desk lamp, it created an intimate atmosphere, making her feel even more nervous to be alone with this incredibly arrogant but oh-so-deliciously hot barefoot man.

Mr. Charbonneau pointed to the broken light at the ceiling. By the challenging look on his face, she could tell that he would not offer any help. Kimberly looked around the room and decided that the desk was her only option.

"You might want to remove your laptop off the desk Sir. I need to move it to change the bulb."

The desk was heavy but Kimberly didn't care. She would not show any weakness now. If the son of the hotel owner wanted to play his silly games, then she'd let him, but she'd make sure to win.

Desk in place, she skipped the chair option and simply pulled herself on top of the desk in one smooth motion.

*Clumsy my ass, Mr. Charbonneau*, she thought.

She was lucky, she'd opted for the pants of her uniform today and not the skirt. Even now, being presented on top of the desk like this under his supervision, made her feel uncomfortable.

Feeling his eyes on her, she focused on the broken light bulb. Up on her tippy toes, she was just tall enough to reach the lamp. Carefully she unscrewed the broken bulb. Then she crouched on the table to take out the new bulb and leave the broken one in its box. As much as she wanted to get out of this room as quickly as possible, she knew that she had to move slowly. She tightened the new bulb in its socket.

*Done.*

In a sporty jump, Kimberly got off the desk and walked to the light switch next to the entrance. She pushed on the switch and the room was flooded with bright light.

*Yes! Yes! Yes!* She smiled triumphantly.

Still not helping, Nicolas Charbonneau stood with crossed arms, watching Kimberly push the heavy desk back to its corner. As if that wasn't enough, he commented.

"You should tuck in your shirt more neatly. Wearing your uniform this sloppy is bad for the hotel's reputation."

Kimberly forced herself to close her mouth.

*Was he for real?*

Quickly she forced a smile back on her face.

"Have a wonderful evening Mr. Charbonneau. If you need anything else, you know how to reach us."

*Wait, just wait,* she thought.

# *Chapter Four*

Kimberly hoped that Nicolas Charbonneau wouldn't depart before she'd have the chance to get back at him. She was ready to risk her job for it. Shift after shift passed by and it almost seemed as if he was avoiding her.

But unless he changed his habits, there was no avoiding her on the early shift as she'd be the only one there at 6:00 AM taking breakfast orders.

When the phone rang as expected, her heart was racing.

"Good morning Mr. Charbonneau. What would you like for breakfast today?"

Kimberly considered it one of her special superpowers to be *extra* friendly to rude guests.

"Coffee, black. Hot milk on the side. Two toasts, wholewheat with olive oil. An avocado, *cubed*. A hard-boiled egg. A banana. And a bottle of the good sparkling water."

*Cubed avocado, how original,* she thought. She had to give it to him, he was quite creative in his ways to test the hotel staff. He probably had already decided beforehand what he would complain about today but he had no idea what was coming for him.

"A pleasure Mr. Charbonneau. Have a wonderful day and please don't hesitate to call us if you need anything else."

Kimberly hung up quickly before she burst out in laughter. After she'd calmed down, she dialed the kitchen's extension.

"James! Our VIP breakfast order just came in. Note it down because it's a little different today."

"Let me guess, he wants the avocado cut up in stars?"

Both started laughing.

"Well, not quite *that* crazy. He wants it *mashed*! And no banana today, he wants *two kiwis* instead. Plus, he ordered water *without* gas! I guess his belly is a bit upset today."

Kimberly giggled.

"Are you serious? He's never had it mashed before."

Kimberly heard the doubt in his voice. "Would you like to call him back and ask yourself?"

"Mashed avocado, kiwis, and water without gas. Got it." James hung up.

*3:0 for Kimberly Jones.*

What a fantastic morning. Kimberly was on a high with a permanent smile planted on her face. When Mr. Charbonneau approached the front desk, her smile didn't vanish but her heart was racing and her stomach did somersaults. She knew she would probably get fired, and lose the job she had instantly loved since she started working at the hotel two months ago. At least though she would get fired with a story to tell. With a small victory and proving that staff didn't need to put up with just anything.

"Good morning Mr. Charbonneau, it's a beautiful day isn't it?"

He leaned on the counter, smiling.

*Why is he smiling?* she wondered.

"I *hate* kiwis," he said, quiet enough for no one else to hear.

*Hates kiwis?* Kimberly cheered silently. That was just what she had hoped for.

She put on her most innocent smile.

"Sir, I don't know what you are talking about but is there anything else I can help you with today?"

His smile stayed put.

"You will pay for this, Ms. Jones!"

There was something about his threat that turned her on. She didn't want to admit it to herself but there was a place between her legs that wasn't pretending. And she couldn't stop herself from wondering if his threat involved her getting spanked over his knee.

When Mr. Charbonneau turned to leave, Kimberly realized why he was smiling. Tucked under his arm, he left the lobby with *her* soccer ball.

*You gotta give it to him, he does have some humor after all.*
*3:1 for Kimberly Jones.*

"I said no!" Kimberly said forcefully and as self-confident as she could manage.

"Come one, how much do you want? Here, take this!"

The sleazy drunk guest who checked in that afternoon threw a bunch of 100$ bills on the counter.

It was close to her shift end but still half an hour to go until the night guard would arrive. There were no other guests in the lobby.

*Why is the security guard always doing his rounds when I need him?* she wondered. Should she call the police?

"Sir, I need you to go to your room. I am *not* interested in you or your money!"

He leaned on the counter and Kimberly got a whiff of his breath smelling like alcohol. She tried to ignore his presence but he lingered at the front desk, like a wild animal who had chased his prey into a corner.

*If he comes an inch closer to me, I'm going to punch him,* she thought.

She pulled her fingers into her palm, forming fists, and tried remembering what she'd learned years ago in a self-defense class. *Convert fear into anger!*

For the first time since Kimberly met Nicolas Charbonneau, she was truly happy to see him approach the front desk.

"The lady said no!"

His voice sounded so threatening, that it gave her the chills.

"Oh come on! You know she wants it, they all do! It's just a matter of finding a price we agree on, isn't that right sweet-".

The hand came flying so fast, that not even Kimberly saw it coming.

*Oh my god, did he really just bitch slap a hotel guest?*

The man dropped to the floor, too drunk to keep his balance. Mr. Charbonneau, who was at least a head taller, towered over him.

"Take your money and go to your room, you are checking out tomorrow or I will have the police kick you out of here!"

The hatred in his voice sent shivers down Kimberly's spine.

As quickly as the man could in his condition, he collected the bills off the front desk and staggered towards the elevator.

Kimberly held her breath the entire time and gasped for air when the elevator door shut closed.

"Are you okay?" Nicolas Charbonneau asked.

"Yes. I think so."

"Are you sure?" The concern in his eyes looked so real. As if he actually cared about her.

*He is an arrogant asshole who hates you and you hate him,* she reminded herself.

But in this very moment, he was her knight in shining armor who came to her rescue.

His eyes had lost all the hardness and Kimberly couldn't stop staring right into them. Her heart rate picked up again but not because of fear this time.

*Why does he have to look so good?*

Kimberly forced herself to look away.

"I better get back to work, I still have a lot to do."

"Of course. I'll stick around, just in case he comes back."

"Thank you," she said and she really meant it. She was relieved that he wouldn't leave her alone. She watched Nicolas Charbonneau walking over to the sofa corner in the lobby. He wore black jeans and a black T-shirt. His hair was still wet.

*Did he just come out of the shower?* He smelled *so* good. And his ass in these jeans looked fantastic.

Mr. Charbonneau turned his head and caught her staring at him. Thankfully he was far enough from her to not see her blush. At least that's what she hoped for.

*Back to work Kimberly.*

Counting the money from the cash register and balancing the credit card payments of the day wasn't an easy task, feeling watched by Mr. Charbonneau. He probably wasn't watching her, but what if he was watching her? Luckily the key cards and registration papers for the next day's arrivals were already coded and printed. She only had to attach them with paper-clips and arrange them in the room number boxes on the wall.

The night guard arrived five minutes early as usual.

"Any late check-ins tonight?" he asked.

"No, everyone's checked in and the cash is balanced. You should have a quiet night." Talking to her colleague, she didn't see Nicolas Charbonneau approaching the front desk for the second time this evening.

"Ms. Jones, I will take you to your car."

His voice startled her.

Kimberly turned around, her heart was about to burst out of her chest.

"I-. My car? I don't have a car. I mean-"

*Calm down, he's being polite after what's happened, that's all.*

"I didn't take my car, I came walking."

"Walking?" His eyes darkened. He didn't seem to like her answer.

"Yes, walking," she answered. "I enjoy walking."

"Grab your stuff, Ms. Jones, I'll *walk* you home then."

It was more of an order than an offer.

*What is his problem?*

"It's really not necessary -"

"I insist!" he cut her off.

The dominant tone of his voice allowed for no further discussion.

*Chapter Six*

They walked silently side by side. The streets were almost empty at this time. The town was touristy but more popular with an older crowd who preferred early morning sightseeing.

Kimberly wondered if she should break the silence but she couldn't come up with anything interesting to say.

"You shouldn't walk here alone at night," he finally started the conversation.

"Doesn't seem to be more dangerous than working late shifts at the best 5-star hotel in town," she countered.

It just came out and she regretted it immediately. She didn't know why but she had the urge to provoke him. He didn't deserve her snappy comment after protecting her from getting assaulted and now simply raising his concern about her safety.

"I will take care of it, you won't have to worry about that anymore."

At least five more minutes passed. The silence grew more and more awkward. Finally, Kimberly couldn't take it anymore.

"So, did you enjoy taking my soccer ball out for some play time?"

Nicolas Charbonneau laughed. A genuine, real laugh.

"Yeah, that was a good one, wasn't it? When I get served mushy avocado, flat water, and disgusting kiwis for breakfast, that's the least I could do to get back at you."

Kimberly smirked and gave him a side look.

*He should laugh more often. Fuck is he fucking hot when he laughs!*

"I really don't know what you're talking about," she said.

She tried her best to not crack up but she couldn't hold back any longer and burst out laughing. Nicolas Charbonneau joined in. They were both laughing together.

. . .

They arrived in front of her building way too fast. She stopped, turning to the man she found arrogant but intriguing, unfriendly yet funny, intimidating, arousing, and incredibly beautiful at the same time.

"Thank you Mr. Charbonneau for accompanying me home. It really wasn't necessary."

"Nicolas."

She met his eyes, the glasses looked so smart on him, giving him that sexy strict teacher look.

"Excuse me?"

"You can call me Nicolas," he repeated more clearly.

*Why do I want to kiss him so badly?*

She hung on to his lips, her heartbeat out of whack and lightnings shooting down to her pussy.

"Thank you, Nicolas. Have a good night."

She lowered her eyes to avoid his intense gaze and turned to leave.

*Please stop me and kiss me.*

She knew she was being ridiculous hoping for something that only happened in romance movies.

Kimberly took a step when a strong hand grabbed her wrist. A thousand electric shocks passed through the spot on her arm where he touched her. As if he had gotten electrocuted himself, he let go of her immediately.

"What shift are you on tomorrow?" he asked.

The spot where he'd touched her still felt hyper-sensitive.

"It's my day off."

Kimberly wondered if she was just imagining it or if Nicolas looked disappointed.

"Enjoy your day off then, you've worked hard for it this week."

He winked at her and then left her standing at her doorstep without looking back.

*You forgot my good night kiss, Mr. Charbonneau.*

She felt silly and excited, happy and horny at the same time.

*Nicolas…. He asked me to call him Nicolas.*

She couldn't believe it. Mr. Arrogant aka Mr. Cubed-Avocado had just offered her to call him by his first name! He also rescued her and then insisted on walking her home. And not only that. They'd laughed out loud together. They'd laughed about secrets that only the two of them shared.

*Nicolas.*

*Chapter Seven*

After last night's events, a day off was the last thing that Kimberly wanted. She stared out of her kitchen window. From there, she could see the rooftop of the hotel.

*Would Jessica get Nicholas's breakfast order right?* Did he give her colleague a hard time as well with his complaints? She felt jealous, thinking about it.

Kimberly hadn't had breakfast herself. She wasn't hungry.

---

Kimberly turned the corner, looking for a parking spot but also searching the beach at the same time.

She was glad that Alicia agreed to meet up with her. Kicking the ball around would be a great distraction and it was about time to fill her best friend in with all the juicy details about Nicolas.

*What are the chances that he is here again?* she wondered. And if he was, would it mean something?

Her heart was beating fast as she tried to convince herself that she wouldn't feel disappointed if he wasn't sitting on the beach chair reading his book.

The honking ripped her out of her thoughts.

*Fuck!* She had almost hit the other car.

Lifting her hand in an apologetic gesture, she continued slowly, keeping her eyes on possible parking spots and not on the beach anymore.

Soccer ball tucked under her arm, Kimberly walked over to the beach.

And there he was.

She spotted him from far away. The same location, in the same beach chair, the same hot guy. He was *her* hot guy, her knight in shining armor.

Kimberly wasn't surprised that he didn't look up when she walked by him. Probably better that way, so he wouldn't notice the groupie type of smile on her face.

*Back to being arrogant today Mr. Charbonneau?* Should

she go over and greet him, now that he had offered her to call him Nicolas?

Alicia was waving from afar, running towards Kimberly from the other direction.

"Oh no Kim, not again. Let's go further down the beach so that this idiot doesn't steal our ball again."

"Nah, don't worry," Kimberly laughed. "Actually, I might try to hit him in the head this time!"

She couldn't wait to explain to her friend that the mystery man was kind of her new boss now.


As expected, Alicia was more than excited about the latest updates concerning Mr. Grumpy. They'd been dissecting his complaints and last night's events for the past hour and weighing out Kimberly's options. Meanwhile, Nicolas neither moved nor spared a look in the girl's direction.

"So you did the kiwi thing and then he left with your soccer ball so now it's your turn again. Do it, shoot the ball!"

Alicia was all giddy, clapping her hands.

"If he gets mad and starts lecturing me again, it'll be your fault. And if he keeps that soccer ball as well, it's your turn to bring the next one to the beach. I'll have none left."

Alicia nodded.

"Deal! Now do it!"

---

Kimberly aimed. Hopefully, her feelings wouldn't get in the way of her skills. She held her breath as she watched the ball fly through the air towards Nicolas.

"Biiiiiiingooooooo!" Alicia cheered, laughing her head off.

The ball hit him right on his hands and he dropped the book. His expression wasn't a friendly one when he lifted his head, looking in their direction.

*4:1 for Kimberly Jones,* she thought.

But all of a sudden didn't feel so self-confident anymore.

She had hoped he'd be happy to see her, that maybe he was at the beach again in the same spot because of her but now her doubts piled up.

*He surely finds me annoying,* she thought.

Despite the slow jog over, her heart was racing. She forced herself to a friendly smile which wasn't easy, considering his stern expression.

"I'm *so* sorry Nicolas. *Very* sorry. You know, it's hard when you're such a clumsy soccer player. The ball just flies off in the wrong direction sometimes."

Nicolas's gaze was intense as he got up slowly and

then picked up the ball at his feet, just like he did last time.

"Tomorrow you work?"

"Yes?"

"On which shift?" His face looked like he was controlling his anger.

"Late shift?"

"Good. I'm expecting you in my room after you finish your shift. Now take your ball and get out of here."

He pushed the ball into her hands, then picked up his book and sat back down.

Kimberly turned around and walked back to Alicia. Her mind was racing, just like her heart.

*I'm expecting you in my room?*

Her pussy twitched at the thought of them being together in his room. Then again, he didn't seem very happy to see her again. No smile, no greeting, just his old, cold, arrogant self. Was firing someone in a hotel room at midnight a thing?

*Chapter Eight*

K imberly stared at the room number 224 on the door. She searched for her courage and tried to collect her thoughts. Since their encounter on the beach more than 24 hours ago, the conversations happening in her head haven't stopped.

She was prepared to argue. Prepared to fight for the fact that what she did in her free time and at work were two completely different things and that her leisure activities should not have any impact on her work contract.

When the light went off in the hallway because there hadn't been any movement for a while, she knew it was time.

*What is the worst thing that can happen?*

The butterflies in her belly went crazy and she felt

her heartbeat up to her throat when she finally lifted her hand to knock on the door.

Nicolas opened the door, only wearing jeans. Barefoot and topless, he looked absolutely delicious, standing in the doorframe.

"Hi."

*Did he really just greet me?* Now that's a first.

Kimberly bit her lip unconsciously. She always did when she was nervous. Nicolas stepped aside, opening the door wide. She walked inside and watched him close the thick old door. As the door shut behind her, Kimberly got goosebumps.

"After you," he said.

She felt his eyes on her as she walked in front of him. The desk lamp was on, the only light source in the room.

*Hopefully, he didn't ask me to come here at this time to change light bulbs again*, she thought.

"Kimberly!"

Her heart stopped. He had never called her by her first name before.

She turned and looked at Nicolas, immediately regretting it, as his intense gaze locked with hers, making her legs go weak. He had that stern expression on his face again.

"The first day we met on the beach, I told you

something. Something I would do if you wouldn't let me read in peace. Do you remember what that was?"

Kimberly's head automatically replayed the first time they met, for what seemed the millionth time.

*If I remember?* she thought, smiling.

She nodded.

"You told me that if I wouldn't turn around and let you read in peace, you would give me a spanking over your knee?"

Repeating his words out loud brought heat to her face and she felt the familiar twitching of her pussy. She was glad it was probably too dark in the room for him to notice.

"That's correct," he said.

Nicolas folded his arms in front of his chest.

"However, yesterday, I got hit *again* by a soccer ball, after previously informing you what would happen, if you didn't let me read in peace. Now you tell me what to do. What do *you* think I should do with you?"

Kimberly felt herself blushing even more but she was feisty enough to hold his intimidating gaze.

"I guess you know the answer yourself Mr. Charbonneau."

"I told you it's *Nicolas* and I want *you* to tell me the answer."

He was glaring at her.

The twitching in her pussy turned to throbbing. This man was too hot to be real. This was like one of her dirty fantasies turning into reality.

"Very well, *Nicolas*." She glared back at him, putting her hands on her hips. "Unless all you do is empty threats, you should take me over your knee and give me a spanking."

Nicolas's mouth twitched, and his serious expression turned to a smile right before he grabbed her wrist.

With Kimberly in tow, he walked over to the desk chair in the corner.

*He's just bluffing,* Kimberly thought. *He won't do it.*

Her heart was racing in her chest and the butterflies in her belly went wild.

Nicolas sat down on the chair and without hesitation, he pulled Kimberly over his knee. She didn't even fight him, she was too surprised that this was actually happening. Her hands touched the cool tiles on the floor instinctively to keep her balance.

Kimberly felt his muscular thighs under her hips as his arm pushed down on her back. And then she waited, distracted only by her pussy's palpitations.

*Why is he hesitating? Did he change his mind?* She knew he was just bluffing. She was so close to living the fantasy she had in her head since the day she met him and now he was chickening out.

"What's wrong Nicolas? Empty threats after all?"

Chapter 9

The slap came down firmly on Kimberly's butt. She gasped, surprised by the feeling of the afterburn his hand left behind. Another slap followed, equally strong, on her other cheek. The fabric of her uniform pants was thin and didn't soften the blow much.

Nicolas grabbed her butt and gave it a squeeze. Then he started.

A firework of slaps rained down on Kimberly's bottom quick and steady. Kimberly felt her body pushed forward with each whack of his solid palm. The spanking was strong enough to leave an impression, heating up her bottom quite quickly.

Kimberly had just started to relax over his knee when Nicolas stopped spanking her.

"Stand up," he ordered.

*That's all?* she wondered. She was a bit disappointed. She knew she could have handled more. Had fantasized about more than that.

Kimberly put a hand on his knee to push herself up. Her shirt had untucked itself and she felt flushed.

"Look at me," he said.

She felt shy when she lifted her head to meet Nicolas's eyes.

"I don't do empty threats."

He smiled. He knew he won this match.

*4:2 for Kimberly Jones.*


"Now take your pants down. Provoking me on purpose deserves a bare bottom spanking."

Kimberly's eyes widened but her pussy throbbed at his words. She had no more doubt now whether he was bluffing or not. His voice sounded more than decisive.

She glared back at Nicolas while opening her pants and pulling them down to her ankles. Then she put her hands back on her hips and lifted her head just a little bit.

*What are you going to do now?* she wondered.

"Panties down too. I said bare bottom."

The sound of his stern voice turned her on like crazy. Nicolas's demand to take off her panties in front of him, made her feel insecure but there was no way she would let him see her weakness.

His eyes, framed by his black glasses, were locked with hers as she hooked her thumbs into the elastic, pulling her panties down slowly. Nicolas made her so nervous that she had to concentrate to not fall over, as she stepped out of her them with her legs feeling like jello.

"Good," he said.

The touch of him taking her hand into his, radiated heat through her body.

"Now get back over my knee Kimberly."

His voice was gentle this time.

She followed the soft pulling of his hand and let him guide her back over his lap. Even though she felt more like covering her face with her hands, she placed them back down on the floor to help her balance. Torn between embarrassment and arousal, she was aware of the view she was giving him.

Nicolas caressed her thighs and then her bottom giving her goosebumps all over her body. His hand felt hot, as he explored her curves. Almost instinctively she opened her legs slightly, to give him access to whatever he wished to explore.

*SMACK!*

Kimberly squeaked in surprise. The sudden contrast from the gentle touch to the sting of his hand, could not have been any stronger.

She hardly recovered from the surprise, catching her breath, when Nicolas continued.

*SMACK! SMACK! SMACK! SMACK!*

Each time his hand came down, Kimberly clenched her teeth together, trying to not make a sound. At the same time, she tried her best to hold still but his spanking did not slow down. Nicolas's hand spanked her perfect soccer butt again and again.

*SMACK! SMACK! SMACK! SMACK*

With each slap, her determination to neither move nor complain decreased. Kimberly's huffing and puffing slowly turned into moaning, accompanied by her legs kicking uncontrollably up in the air. Nicolas seemed to have no problem holding her in place with his arm wrapped tightly around her wrist.

When he planted three hard spanks in a row, Kimberly's hand flew back, rubbing her right butt cheek.

He was nice enough to grant her a little break, but before she knew it, he grabbed her hand and locked it with his own in the small of her back.

"I'm not done with you yet," he said.

Kimberly's heart sped up. Here she was, getting spanked by the man who had driven her crazy in all sorts of ways since the day she met him. Since the day he threatened to do exactly that. Take her over his knee and spank her. And she wanted it. Fantasized about it each and every day since. But how much more could she take?

With ease, he lifted her up a little, shifting her enough to push his right leg between her thighs. Then the spanking continued but it had just gotten a little sweeter. While she couldn't move and kick as much anymore, the smacks now pushed her onto his leg, putting pressure on her pussy each time.

When Nicolas finally stopped, his hand rested on her very sore bottom. She was out of breath. He released her other hand and Kimberly put it back on the floor. Her backside felt hot and tingly all over.

Nicolas rubbed her skin gently and it felt amazing. Slowly her breathing slowed down and so did her heartbeat as she relaxed over his knee.

The warmth of her cheeks radiated everywhere and the throbbing in her pussy picked up again.

*I can't believe I just got spanked,* she thought. As much as she'd wanted him to stop spanking her just a few moments ago, she already missed his firm touch. That incredible feeling of him being in control and her having no other option than submitting to Nicolas.

She couldn't hold back a moan, when his finger suddenly slipped between her cheeks, drawing an invisible line along her slit. Nicolas pulled her butt cheeks apart and then moments passed, with Kimberly spread open and exposed at his disposal.

She held her breath, torn back and forth between feeling embarrassed but aroused like never before.

Finally, he released her butt cheeks and started exploring her pussy instead.

"I've been wanting to do this to you since the day I met you," he said, slipping a finger into her.

*Chapter 10*

His muscular leg rubbed against her pussy, while his finger repeatedly pushed inside of her. Kimberly's moans grew louder. Covered with her juices, his finger easily slipped out of her pussy and moved up her bottom to explore the tight hole above.

Kimberly's eyes widened in surprise.

"Don't!"

Her hand flew back, trying to cover her most private area. Nicolas gently took her hand and moved it aside.

"Just relax and enjoy. I won't put anything inside of you. Not today."

*Not today?* Kimberly thought.

His finger went back into her wet pussy, just to pull it out and move back up to tease her tight hole.

Kimberly took a deep breath but she didn't stop him this time.

He circled around it, his moistened finger brushing across the highly sensitive spot. Kimberly had never let anyone touch her there. She was surprised about how good it felt. Good but dirty. Dirty and wrong. But oh so good.

Nicolas's thumb applied just a slight amount of pressure on her shy booty hole, while his other hand went back to rub her pussy.

Spread out over his leg with her buttocks still feeling on fire and neither knowing nor wanting to know where his fingers were rubbing and pushing inside of her, the orgasm shook aggressively through her body.

Instead of slowing down, Nicolas firmly grabbed her sore butt cheek and then pushed two fingers inside her pussy, fucking her hard with his hand. Within seconds she tipped over for a second time.

Kimberly pushed herself against his leg, squeezing her thighs together as she felt her pussy contract again and again.

Nicolas gently rubbed her bottom and legs, giving her heart finally a chance to slow down. But with her arousal satisfied, the embarrassment kicked back in.

Kimberly was suddenly aware of how she had let herself go in front of Nicolas Charbonneau.

He didn't just see her naked, he saw her spread out like a starfish draped over his knee. And he touched everything. *Everything.*

Kimberly blushed, thinking of it. She needed to get up. Get dressed.

Nicolas steadied her to get back to her feet. He picked up her clothes from the floor and handed them over. She was just closing the button of her pants when he held a glass of ice-cold sparkling water in front of her. The cool beverage felt wonderful down her throat which had dried up from breathing heavily this whole time. The bubbles tickled her tongue. She wasn't used to drinking gasified water. It felt good, almost like a glass of champagne, only more refreshing.

"Come, I'll take you home." He took the empty glass from her, leaving it on the desk.

They walked the whole way without talking, both caught up in their thoughts. Approaching her building she knew she needed to say something, something to make him stay, to continue whatever it was between them.

Did he want more? She definitely wanted more, the taste he had just given her, made her want to finish the whole buffet. Made her want to try everything he had to offer and then repeat again and again.

"I wasn't completely honest with you," she started.

He kept on walking while looking at her sideways.

"It was me changing your breakfast order," she admitted.

She kept her eyes on the sidewalk in front of her.

Nicolas stopped abruptly, turning towards her. His finger lifted her chin up to face him. She wanted to drown in his dark, mysterious eyes.

"So you've lied to me?"

His voice was strict but the corners of his mouth were twitching suspiciously.

"I did," she answered, lowering her eyelashes in fake remorse.

"If *accidentally* hitting me with a soccer ball results in you ending up over my knee, what kind of punishment do you think *lying* will lead to?"

Kimberly smirked at his sarcastic way of pronouncing *accidentally*, both of them well aware that it had never been an accident.

"Please tell me," she begged, biting her lip, waiting for him to sentence her for another sweet punishment. But instead, his hand moved around the back of her head and pulled her into a kiss.

His mouth was hungry, his tongue exploring her roughly, claiming her mouth. Luckily he steadied her with his other hand when her knees buckled. He grabbed her butt, pulling her so close that she could feel his erection hard against her belly. Nicolas left her breathless and wet between her legs when he pulled away from her mouth.

"I won't tell you, but you will find out."

With his threat in the air, he left her standing, left her wanting, left her pussy wet, open and ready for him.

She looked after Nicolas, longing for his touch but he walked away, not turning around.

Kimberly was distracted at work. Every time the elevator door opened, she glanced over to see if Nicolas was coming out.

*What punishment do you think lying will lead to?*

She couldn't get his words out of her head. His voice, sometimes soft, sometimes strict. The mix of it. It made her wet again just thinking of it. She had been lying awake until early morning, wondering what punishment he could have in mind. Now at work, her mind kept on slipping off to dream of last night.

*Will he ask me to come to his room again?* she wondered.

Would he ask her today or would he keep her waiting, making her suffer?

"Kimberly!"

Jessica startled her, interrupting her daydreams.

"Sorry, what did you say?"

Jessica laughed.

"A penny for your thoughts?"

Kimberly blushed, making Jessica laugh even more.

She had to get herself under control. Preparing the check-ins for the next day was a good distraction. It was a repetitive task, coding the key cards for the rooms and printing the registration papers. She was forced to concentrate, writing down the room numbers on the little cardboard envelopes for each key card. Kimberly took the next envelope and started writing Room 224 on it.

*Room 224?*

The realization that Nicolas would have to check out in order for new guests to check into his room, hit her like a ton of bricks.

"Mr. Charbonneau is leaving tomorrow," she said more to herself than Jessica.

Saying it out loud made it more real. The thought of him not being there anymore by this time tomorrow twisted her stomach.

Jessica looked at Kimberly.

"You really have your head in the clouds today. Haven't you heard yet? He checked out this morning at 5:00 AM. Fabulous if you ask me, no more changing light bulbs and other bullying games we have to put up with."

*He left? At 5:00 AM?*

As Kimberly tried to process the new information, the knot in her stomach twisted even tighter and her eyes started burning.

"Kimberly, are you okay? You're really totally weird today."

"Yes-. No-. Yes-. I'm just -, a bit nauseous." Kimberly blinked back her tears. Her nose suddenly felt stuffed.

She left running, so Jessica wouldn't see her tears gushing out already.

Locking herself in the staff's bathroom, she dropped to the floor leaning against the door. Save from anyone's looks, she finally let her tears flow freely.

Kimberly muffled her cries in the perfectly bleached white sleeve of her blouse. She took deep breaths to calm herself down, telling herself he wasn't worth crying over but the spasms in her chest just wouldn't stop. The mere thought of him made her body shake, and it was impossible to hold back the crying that emerged from deep inside.

*Am I merely another notch on his bedpost?*

A stupid game to see if the employee would submit? Had she really been naive enough to think it could have meant as much to him as it meant to her?

***

Kimberly forced herself to go back to work the next day. Calling in sick because of a broken heart was unacceptable. She owed herself this much dignity after acting so naive and letting herself be tricked into such a vulnerable position.

She was shocked at how much Nicolas had affected her. How was it possible to develop such deep feelings for someone while she'd loathed him so much?

Kimberly twisted and turned the situation to make sense of it. It was true, he threatened her with a spanking the first time they met and he just pulled through with his promise nothing more.

*But why did he kiss me?*

That kiss wasn't just a kiss. No one had ever kissed her like that before. There was passion. Longing.

Was it purely physical? Did he kiss everyone like that?

Kimberly had to push the thoughts of Nicolas kissing other women away quickly. But pushing all thoughts of him away turned out way more difficult than she thought.

Instead of being distracted at work, everything reminded her of *him*. The spot where he stood the first morning ordering his peculiar breakfast. The sofa in the lobby he sat on, watching over her after saving her from the drunk guest. Even the front desk's telephone, on which she had received more internal phone calls than ever, while Nicolas was staying at the hotel.

"Feeling better?" Jessica asked.

"Yes, much better, thanks for taking over for me yesterday."

"Excuse me, I'm looking for Ms. Jones?"

Kimberly looked up.

The man in blue overalls pulled a silver suitcase but he didn't look like a guest.

"That would be me, how can I help you, Sir?"

*Chapter 12*

"I'm here to install a panic button at the front desk. I was told you would be in charge of telling me where the best spot would be for it?"

Kimberly's heart started pounding so hard in her chest, it hurt. She knew who was behind this. Nicolas had told her he would make sure that nobody at the front desk would ever have to worry about being in danger again.

He kept his promise.

But why did he even care if he didn't care about her? Was this one of his bullying techniques? The least he could do was to leave her in peace now.

She had to push away the thoughts. She had to stop thinking about him. Once and for all.

Not even her days off gave her much joy. Kimberly canceled on Alicia. She didn't feel like playing soccer on the beach. Something else that would only remind her of *him*.

It sucked.

Everything sucked.

Why did he need to show up in her life when everything had been so perfect without him?

She had been debating with herself for days now if she should write to him or not. A quick search on the Internet came up with the contact email of his software firm in no time.

*He owes me an explanation*, Kimberly thought.

It's been a week since he kissed her. The hope that maybe he left her some kind of secret message, so that no one at the hotel would find out about their relationship, had lingered around for a few days. But now, a week later, she knew he wouldn't reach out to her.

She tried to find closure but she just couldn't without knowing what happened. Did she do something wrong?

She needed to know.

*"Fuck it,"* she thought out loud and then opened the email app on her phone.

. . .

*Nicolas,*
*Would a goodbye have been too much to ask for?*
*Kimberly*


Kimberly pressed send.
That was it.
She did it.
Nothing to lose.
Her heart was already broken.

---

When the email from Nicolas Charbonneau showed up in her inbox, Kimberly wasn't too sure anymore if reaching out to him had been a good idea. This whole time she waited for a message from him and now that she held his reply in her hands, she somehow felt too scared to read it. Her hands were sweaty, holding her phone. Taking a deep breath, she opened the email.


*Dear Kimberly,*

*I'm very sorry but I realized that I crossed a line I should have never crossed.*

*Engaging with an employee of my father's hotel was extremely unprofessional and I feel ashamed that I took advantage of you. That's why I left without saying goodbye.*

*It's better this way.*

*N.*

Kimberly must have re-read the message a hundred times. His explanation made no sense at all.

Hadn't she been part of this decision? He didn't take advantage of her. She wanted to cross the line with him.

In fact, she wanted him from the moment she saw him on the beach before she even knew who he was. Her confusion turned into rage.

*Is he seriously using his Daddy as an excuse to disappear without a word?*

There was no possible excuse for spanking someone, fingering someone, kissing someone, making promises to someone, and then literally ghosting them.

He was an arrogant asshole. He had always been one. He never even hid that fact and she still fell for him.

It was her own fault. She was a stupid and naive

girl who had been too impressed by the first man coming along who wasn't afraid to take her over his knee.

*Time to stop caring, Kimberly! Get your fucking shit together. He's not worth it!*

Chapter 13

Managing corporate events at the local banquet hall was a real dream job. Two months ago, she had accepted the new position, leaving the hotel behind. Finally, Kimberly had weekends off, like other *normal* people.

Throwing herself 120% into her new job almost let her forget about Nicolas Charbonneau.

Almost.

Working mostly with businessmen, there was no lack of attention of the opposite gender and she truly enjoyed it. One thing was clear for her though, that she would *never* engage with someone at work again. She had learned that lesson the hard way.

Lying alone in bed at night, Kimberly did allow herself to think back to the evening in room 224 with Nicolas. How he grabbed her wrist. How he demanded that she pull down her panties. How he spanked her hard and then fingered her gently, exploring places no one had ever explored.

Enough time had passed to think of that night without feeling sad. She masturbated thinking of him and that was okay because she was using him.

At least that's what she told herself.

Finding parking close to the beach on a Saturday was quite the challenge. It was one of those sacrifices that came with her new Monday-to-Friday job.

The beach would be packed as well, not a lot of space to kick the ball today but Alicia and she didn't need much. Worst case, they would be like everyone else and just lie around lazyily on their towels.

Walking towards the beach, Kimberly felt anxious today. Arriving at the boardwalk she realized why.

She spotted him right away.

The same place, the same beach chair, and *her* soccer ball next to him in the sand.

Her heart immediately started racing and she had a hard time breathing all of a sudden.

"He's here," is all she said to Alicia.

Alicia's eyes widened.

"Fuck Kimberly, I'm sorry, shall we go somewhere else?"

"Nah, this is our beach, we've been here first. And I'm over him. We're staying."

She tried to sound cool and in control of her emotions but who was she kidding? It was more of a pep talk to herself trying to calm down her racing heart. And Alicia, who had to listen to most of her crying and whining about him, knew her better than anyone else. There was no reason to hide her true feelings in front of her but she was too proud to admit how excited she was about Nicolas being there.


"Kim! He's walking towards us!" Alicia whispered.

*Fuck, Fuck, Fuck!*

Kimberly sat on her beach towel, with her back towards Nicolas. When he stopped in front of her, his shadow covered her.

Knowing he was coming, at least gave her the chance to not be completely caught off guard.

"Excuse me, you're blocking my sun!" she said.

It was the first thing that came to her mind.

Glancing up at him was a mistake. The response of her body was intense. The blood rushed through her veins and the butterflies went crazy in her belly.

"You quit?"

*Chapter 14*

**H**is voice! She had forgotten what his stern voice did to her.

*Fuck!*

She needed to calm down. The last thing she wanted was for him to see how much he affected her.

"I did," she answered.

*Don't say more than you have to*, she told herself.

"I hope I had nothing to do with that decision?"

*Yes, you asshole, it's all your fault!*

"Oh no, of course not. A great career opportunity came up for me, that's all."

Nicolas looked down at her, searching for her eyes. Kimberly looked away quickly. She couldn't meet his eyes without everything bubbling to the surface again. She had to keep her cool.

"I came to give you your soccer ball back," he said.

"Keep it, it's a sweet reminder for you that you still owe me."

*Fuck! Why did I say this? Where did this come from? Now he thinks I'm still interested.*

Nicolas's smile grew wider. He looked gorgeous in his black beach shorts, matching his black glasses.

She stared at his muscular thighs. The thigh she rubbed herself on when he had her spread out like a starfish on top of him.

He winked at her.

"You're right, there is still unfinished business I need to take care of."

He said bye to Alicia and went back to his spot on the beach, with the soccer ball under his arm.

While her pussy was over the top excited, Kimberly wanted to stick her head in the sand.

*What the fuck did I just do?*

Did she really just flirt with the guy who left her hanging? Who left without saying goodbye? Who used her, made her do the most intimate things she's ever done, and then dropped her like a hot potato?

"Are you okay?" Alicia brought her back into the moment.

Kimberly covered her face with her hands and screamed quietly into them.

To avoid passing Nicolas on the beach, she took an extra detour walking to her car. Her efforts didn't pay off. She saw him from far, leaning against her red old car.

She decided to ignore his presence, opened the trunk, and threw her things inside without sparing a look at him. When she went to open the driver's door, Nicolas blocked her way.

"What do you want from me?" she snapped.

For once Nicolas didn't look as confident and in control as usual.

"I want you."

His words made her cringe.

"How dare you show up here after two months, saying shit like that? You left without a word Nicolas! And now you're arrogant enough to think you could impress me, telling me you want me? You really think I'm so naive to jump at you at the first opportunity?"

She felt furious.

What was he thinking?

"You asked me a question and I've answered it honestly, that's all. I'm really sorry. I regret leaving like I did but I can't turn back time now."

Kimberly stared at him, not saying anything.

*That's all?* she wondered. And now he thinks that I

come crawling back to him? She wanted him to say the right thing. She wanted him to give her a reason. She *so* wanted to believe that what he said was true. But how could she possibly?

"Look, Kimberly, if you can look into my eyes and tell me that you haven't thought of me, that you haven't fantasized about the night in the hotel room, that you haven't thought of our kiss every single day, then I will leave you alone and not bother you anymore."

She looked up at him, into his dark eyes, determined to lie. To tell him that she *never* thought of him and that the kiss meant nothing.

Her mouth opened.

The sentence was already formed in her head, the words ready on the tip of her tongue, but they just wouldn't come out.

Kimberly turned her head. She couldn't stand letting him see her weakness. He didn't deserve to know any of her feelings, just to take advantage of her again.

"Would it make a difference telling you that I've had mashed avocado every single day since I've left, just because it reminds me of you?" he asked.

Kimberly tried to keep a straight face but his confession made the corners of her mouth twitch.

She looked down at her feet when his hand lifted

up her chin, forcing her to look at him. Just like he did the last time she saw him on that evening, right before he kissed her.

His touch and then looking into his eyes brought back a flood of memories and emotions. The electricity was still there, there was no denying it. Her body was a traitor who didn't know how to pretend to not care.

Nicholas's expression was dead serious.

"And I still don't like it mashed. It's weird, you know? Like eating Guacamole for breakfast."

Kimberly couldn't help it but laugh. His closeness made her feel happy, nervous, and scared at the same time.

She wasn't ready to forgive him but she was willing to hear him out.

"So, what do you say? Would you join me for dinner this evening?" he asked.

Kimberly immediately missed his touch, when his hand released her chin.

"I'm not into fancy restaurants," she answered.

"7:00 PM. I'll pick you up in front of your building."

Nicolas didn't wait for an answer. He didn't leave her an opportunity to say no. He had decided for her. And just like he'd done it before, he left her standing there, alone again, feeling chilly despite the hot day.

*You arrogant piece of shit,* she thought.

But she felt happy. She hadn't felt this happy since the night in his room.

"How's the fancy food?" Nicolas asked.

Kimberly answered by biting passionately into her BLT, while looking into his eyes and letting out a deep moan.

It was the perfect mix of soft and crunchy with just the right amount of extra mayonnaise in it.

His face hardened.

"Stop moaning! You're going to give me an erection."

"Is that so?"

Holding his gaze, she grabbed a sweet potato fry, dipped it into the spicy chipotle mayo, and bit into it. Then she closed her eyes, letting out another moan.

"Stop it or I'll spank you right here in front of everyone."

This time it was Kimberly who got aroused. Hearing the word *spank* out of Nicolas's mouth, immediately gave her a flashback of being bent over his knee. But getting spanked in front of everyone in the restaurant?

No. It was better to not take a chance. There was no doubt he would pull through with his threat.

"Ok, ok, I'll stop."

His face softened as he took a bite of his own BLT.

Despite the playful atmosphere, Kimberly kept on getting distracted by the little voice in her head. As much as she enjoyed all the sparks and spiciness that was going on between them, she was scared to get hurt again.

*Don't fall for him, he'll break your heart twice,* she warned herself.

What did he want from her? Was he looking for a booty call while he was in town?

"Would you have asked me to go out for dinner if I was still working at the hotel?"

Nicolas looked at her, his face serious.

"Yes."

She didn't believe him.

"So, suddenly you don't care anymore about the

hotel's reputation and what your father would say if he found out what things you did to his staff?"

Nicolas laughed.

"I *really* hope my father *never* finds out what exactly I did to you."

His eyes sparkled.

Kimberly covered her face with her hands so that Nicolas wouldn't see her blushing but he pulled her wrists gently to the side to uncover her face.

"Jokes aside. I found a different solution. I told my Dad that I wouldn't be testing his hotels anymore and that he should hire someone else. And I booked myself into a different hotel in town. Finding out that you quit was an added bonus, I guess."

It took a moment for Kimberly to process all the information.

"You quit your father's business?" she asked.

"I've never worked for my father, I just did him a favor by staying at the hotel every now and then, testing the customer service quality. It was fun and definitely *very* entertaining watching you change the light bulb in my room. But-. It was also exhausting playing the bad guy all the time and knowing that everyone there hates me. I'm glad I don't have to go back."

Kimberly looked at him for a long time. There were no alarm bells ringing in her head right now.

She believed him and knowing that he had looked for a solution to be with her, made her heart skip a beat.

---

Nicolas sipped on his coffee.

"So? Is the milk hot enough?" She couldn't stop teasing him.

"No, it's not!" He lifted his hand to wave over the waitress.

Kimberly pulled his arm down in a panic.

"Don't!" she hissed.

The most mischievous smile lightened up Nicolas's face.

"I was just kidding. Believe it or not, I'm *not* the complaining type of customer at restaurants or hotels."

It was already dark when they left the diner.

"Come, let's take a walk," Nicolas said, taking Kimberly's hand in his as if it were the most normal thing in the world.

They walked towards the beach and then took the boardwalk.

Especially on Saturday, it was a popular spot for people to go for a stroll after dinner and eat ice cream. The orange streetlights made everything look softer and a little bit romantic. The humid warm sea breeze smelled salty. A street musician played the Spanish guitar, singing love songs. It was the kind of atmosphere that was hopelessly depressing if you were alone.

But Kimberly wasn't alone. Her fingers intertwined with the fingers of her mystery man from the beach. A man who made her cry, who made her laugh, who made her feel insecure yet safe at the same time.

They weren't talking much. Kimberly wished she could freeze the moment, and make the evening last forever.

Eventually, they reached the spot next to the beach where she saw Nicolas for the first time. By the way, how he looked over to the spot on the beach where the girls always played soccer, she could tell that he thought of it as well.

Nicolas slowed down and then stopped walking.

"I've got you something."

He lifted the small plastic bag in his hand.

Kimberly had been wondering what he carried around this whole time but didn't want to come off as nosy.

He handed her the bag.

"Go ahead, look inside."

Kimberly had no idea what to expect. What could Nicolas possibly have gotten her? The bag was too small and too light to have her soccer ball in it.

She slipped her hand into the bag and pulled out a toothbrush.

*A toothbrush?*

"Sorry, but is this a polite way of telling me that I have bad breath?" Kimberly asked.

She looked perplexed at the purple toothbrush.

"Are you serious?" Nicolas asked, with a stern look on his face. "Give it to me!" he ordered, literally ripping it out of her hand.

Kimberly's mouth opened in astonishment when Nicolas, toothbrush in hand, went down on one knee in front of her.

He cleared his throat and looked into her eyes.

"Kimberly Jones, please accept this toothbrush as a token of my deep affection. Would you do me the honor of spending the night at the hotel with me?"

Kimberly covered her mouth with one hand, hiding the crazy grin on her face.

*Could this man be any sweeter?* How could she say no to this invitation?

She took the toothbrush from his hands.

"The honor is all mine, Nicolas Charbonneau. I would be delighted."

Nicolas got up from his kneeling position and pulled Kimberly into his arms.

His arms felt right around her. She could spend the rest of her life hugging Nicolas. She was on her tippy toes, resting her face in the nook of his shoulder and neck. He smelled *so* good. The smell reminded her of the first time she brought coffee to his room and he came out of the shower naked, only covered by a towel.

She couldn't tell who turned their head first. Who initiated it. But it felt natural when their lips met.

He kissed her so gently.

Nicolas moved slowly, his lips soft on hers. It made it feel even more intense. The perfect kiss to accompany his romantic proposal.

When they finally let go of each other, Kimberly realized that there was still something inside the plastic bag she held. Putting her hand back inside, she pulled out a beautiful wooden hairbrush.

"Oh! Thank you, that's so sweet of you but I don't really use hairbrushes. My curls are low maintenance, I usually just finger comb through them."

Nicolas had that mischievous smile on his face again.

"Who said that it's for your hair?"

When it dawned on her what he was implying, she felt all hot and fidgety, staring at the wooden brush in her hand.

*Did he really? Would he really?*

Nicolas didn't hesitate to confirm her suspicion.

"You left me your soccer ball as a sweet reminder that I still owe you something and you are right. Remember that little incident where you lied to me?"

*How did he do this? How did he get her wet with just words?* she wondered.

The blood pulsated between her legs and

Kimberly's hands felt sweaty. Somehow he knew the perfect recipe to make her nervous, excited, and curious at the same time.

"My hotel is right here around the corner. What do you say?"

Kimberly looked down at the wooden hairbrush in her hand, touching the smooth surface of it. She could already see it in action, the fantasy playing out in front of her eyes. Looking back at Nicolas, she took his hand and put the hairbrush into it.

"Let's go, what are you waiting for?" she asked.

Then she grabbed his free hand and pulled him to start walking.

*Chapter 17*

The hotel room wasn't just a room, it was a junior suite with a huge window facing the sea. The door had hardly closed, when Nicolas pushed Kimberly against the wall.

His kiss wasn't gentle this time, it was hungry and rough. His left hand fixed her wrist against the wall while the other grabbed her butt and squeezed it. His thigh was pushing between her legs, making Kimberly moan into his mouth.

He knew how to press all the right buttons and her body responded accordingly.

Her free hand slipped underneath his T-shirt to touch his skin. He felt burning hot. She pulled him closer, to feel him even more intensely, to increase the push between her legs. When Nicolas pulled away from her, they were both breathing heavily.

"Stop distracting me, Kimberly. First you'll get punished and then I will pleasure you."

Her panties were soaked already but hearing him say *punished*, didn't help that situation.

Just like the first time, Nicolas grabbed her by the wrist and pulled her to the other end of the room where the sofa was. He opened Kimberly's jeans shorts. With one firm move, he pulled them down, together with her panties. She was way too horny to feel shy about it today.

"Step out of your clothes," he said.

His voice was stern but reassuring at the same time.

Kimberly eagerly followed his demand, removing the jeans and panties which were wrapped around her ankles. She wanted so badly for him to touch her but instead, he removed the hairbrush out of his back pocket, sat down on the sofa, and then manhandled her with ease over his lap.

Bent over his knee, she could feel the cool breeze of the A/C on her exposed pussy.

Nicolas took his time. He touched her thighs, glided his hand along her curves, and eventually slid his hand down her slit, feeling the wetness between her legs. His gentle touch gave her goosebumps, sending shivers through her body.

A little slap made her butt jiggle.

"Open!" he ordered.

She spread her legs a little wider and Nicolas took the opportunity to slide a finger into her. Kimberly moaned as her pussy clenched tightly around the unexpected intruder. Her cunt felt so needy and empty as his finger slid back out, leaving her wanting.

*SLAP. SLAP. SLAP. SLAP.*

The rhythmic slaps landing on her bottom were light. It didn't hurt, they just made her bottom vibrate non-stop. She could feel the vibrations in her pussy, making her wonder if she could actually have an orgasm only from being spanked like this.

Every now and then Nicolas took a break and grabbed her cheeks. Not soft, not hard, just a firm loving squeeze. He went back and forth between rubbing, caressing, and spanking her bottom. It was pure bliss.

*I could do exactly this for the rest of my life,* Kimberly thought.

She felt so deeply relaxed, almost hypnotized.

Every touch of his hand felt so incredible that she didn't even protest this time when his finger started exploring her ass. On the contrary, she didn't want him to stop. She wanted to do dirty things with Nicolas. She *wanted* him to push her boundaries, forcing her to try the things she was too scared to ask for.

He chuckled as Kimberly spread her legs more. She didn't need much to cum already.

"You forgot something, Kimberly. As much as I love playing with your ass, I still need to punish you for lying to me."

Feeling the cool wood of the hairbrush gliding across her warmed-up backside made her feel a little bit nervous.

As if he could read her mind, his free hand took hers, giving it a reassuring squeeze. She smiled, holding onto his warm hand.

Then he started.

His hand lifted and Kimberly held her breath.

The smack of the brush brought her curves back into vibration.

Relieved, she exhaled. It wasn't too bad. More stingy than the gentle spanking before but less painful than two months ago when he had spanked her hard with his hand.

*SMACK. SMACK. SMACK. SMACK.*

The wooden brush quickly covered every spot of her butt, coming down on her again and again.

When Nicolas smacked both her upper thighs, Kimberly yelped surprised, and wriggled on his lap. The brush definitely had a wicked punch on those sensitive spots.

"Ready?" he asked.

His words confirmed her suspicion that the spanking so far had only been a warm-up. Her heart started racing immediately.

*Will I be able to handle it?* she wondered.

She squeezed his hand, doubting she could ever be ready for what was coming. But she wanted this. She had wanted this from the moment she met Nicolas.

The day he threatened her, he brainwashed her for good. Ever since she'd never been able to fantasize about anything else but him spanking and fucking her.

Kimberly groaned loud when the first *real* whack of the hairbrush hit her butt.

*Holy moly that stings,* she thought. But luckily the sting transformed quickly back into pleasant tingling.

Nicolas paused, giving her time to prepare for the next.

*SMACK!*

The sound and Kimberly's moan echoed in the hotel suite.

*Hopefully, the room is soundproof*, she thought.

After two more hard smacks, Nicolas put the brush down on her back, to rub her butt gently. His other hand never let go of holding hers.

Kimberly spread her legs automatically, to give him full access to her body. He rewarded her with a soft rub of her pussy, making her moan in pleasure this time. But his sweet treatment didn't even last a minute.

He picked up the hairbrush from her back again and then her punishment continued.

The brush hit her on the left, came down on the right, and paused for a second before starting all over again. The rhythm was slow enough for the aftermath of the sting to develop but too fast to get a break from it. Once the burn was lessening on one side, the other cheek was at its hottest point.

The constant whacks coming down with no mercy, had Kimberly squirming on Nicolas's lap. He squeezed her hand in support while increasing the force of Kimberly's punishment just a tad more. She wriggled, twisted, and turned, her legs in constant movement.

When she thought she couldn't take more, Nicolas stopped.

*Is he done?* she wondered.

Her butt felt on fire.

"Your bottom looks absolutely beautiful, it's literally glowing!"

His voice had lost all sternness. His hand touched her sensitive skin gently.

"Go lie down on the bed," he said and helped her up from her position.

---

The contrast of the cool lotion dripping on her burning butt surprised Kimberly. The soreness of her skin improved immediately.

But even more comforting was the way Nicolas touched her. His big hands, which could be so firm, were now gentle and soft. He spread the lotion over her bottom in smooth strokes. Both hands worked simultaneously down to her thighs, legs, and feet.

"Take your shirt off," he said and then helped her get out of it.

Adding more lotion, he massaged her back as well. It was a firm massage just like Kimberly loved it, but whenever Nicolas moved close to her bottom, his massage turned into gentle strokes, hardly touching the surface of her skin.

He was in no rush, taking his sweet time but

finally, he ended up where both Kimberly and Nicolas wanted him to end up, with his hands sliding up her inner thighs, to the warmth between her legs.

Kimberly moaned. She felt more relaxed than she had ever felt in her life. His fingers softly stroked her pussy, exploring the swollen mound. She wondered if all her blood had accumulated in her cunt, because she felt as if she was about to burst.

"Turn," he said, touching her shoulder.

Turning around and looking at Nicolas, she realized that he was still fully dressed, while she was lying completely naked on the bed. She watched him taking in her body and felt shy under his visual examination yet too aroused to protest. All she wanted was for him to touch her.

"Please," she begged.

Kimberly took his hand and guided him back between her legs. Not being touched by him anymore was pure torture.

Nicolas smiled at her, leaving his hand where Kimberly put it but without moving it. She got more and more impatient, spreading her legs, and winding herself a little, just to feel his hand move on her pussy.

"I want you to come when I fuck you, not before, so you will have to control yourself a little," he said.

"Then please, fuck me now! Please. I want you!"

She lifted her hips to push against his hand.

Nicolas chuckled.

"I could definitely get used to you begging me to fuck you."

Nicolas lay down on the bed, his head between her legs. Grabbing her thighs, he pulled Kimberly closer to his lips and then pushed her thighs apart a little further to give him full access.

His tongue slid along her slit, poking and probing to find her sweet spot. When he discovered her clit under the swollen lips, he licked her softly. His tongue drove Kimberly almost crazy. She pushed on his head between her legs and he took the clue, sucking and licking her clit harder. And to drive her even crazier, he started fingering her at the same time.

Kimberly arched her back, spreading her legs wider.

This was it.

She was so close. So close to releasing all the tension. The tension of seeing Nicolas again on the beach. Of him waiting at her car not taking no for an answer. Of him threatening her with a spanking during dinner. Of her unpacking the hairbrush, knowing she would be punished with it. Of the fear it would hurt too much and the arousal when he used it on her.

When Kimberly thought, it couldn't get any

better Nicolas pushed with his thumb against her tight asshole. With her pussy being fucked by his finger, her clit getting licked by his tongue and his thumb putting pressure on her forbidden hole, Kimberly lost control.

Her moan was stretched out, accompanying the waves of ecstasy that rushed through her body. Kimberly's legs closed around his head and then pushed Nicolas away, as her clit became too sensitive.

*Holy fuck! That was by far, the best orgasm of my life!* she thought.

She was breathing heavily with a huge smile on her face.

Nicolas leaned over Kimberly and whispered in her ear.

"I told you to control yourself. I told you to come when I fuck you, not before. Why do you keep on giving me reasons to spank you?"

Kimberly couldn't believe him.

"You can't blame me for coming when you do what you did to me. That's not fair."

"Get on your knees," he ordered.

*Is he serious? Is he really going to spank me again?*

*Chapter 19*

S lowly, she pushed herself up and turned around to get on her hands and knees. She could only imagine the view she was giving Nicolas right now.

To her relief, she heard Nicolas take off his pants and the noise of a condom wrapper. She felt him getting back on the bed behind her, and then two fingers pushed without a warning into her.

"Still nice and wet. That's how I always want you to be. Ready for me to fuck you."

Nicolas's words turned her on even more. The whole situation was just too good to be real.

When his dick pushed against her, her lips parted. Nicolas stretched her out slowly, inch by inch until he was all the way in. Kimberly tilted her hips until he could not go any deeper.

He was big but she felt so aroused that her pussy quickly adjusted to his size.

As slow as he'd pushed inside of her, he pulled back out, his cock leaving an empty void.

"Ready?" he asked.

Kimberly nodded.

And then he started fucking her.

Fucking her good, fucking her hard, fucking her like her wet and needy pussy wanted to get fucked. Kimberly had to put her hands in front of her on the bed to not lose balance, to not tip over from Nicolas's loins thrashing against her bottom.

Not only did he perfectly hit her G-Spot in this position, but the rough pounding made her sore butt burn all over again.

It felt incredible.

The thrusts got harder and harder and the slapping sound of skin hitting skin added to Kimberly's arousal.

What made her tip over for the second time this evening, was when Nicolas's dick swelled substantially thicker, coming inside of her. Even through the thin layer of the condom, she felt the burst of sperm shooting out.

*Best feeling ever.*

Kimberly was cuddled up in Nicolas's arms. Showered and still naked they were lying on the piled-up pillows of the king-size bed.

"You know what's crazy?" Kimberly asked.

Nicolas turned his head to kiss her forehead. "You tell me."

"I just got hungry again," she said.

"You know what's even crazier? Me too! Let's order some food then."

Kimberly was excited. She'd worked at the hotel and brought food to the guest's rooms a couple of times but she'd never used room service in a hotel herself before.

"Do you have a menu? Do you actually think the kitchen is still open at this time?"

Her stomach rumbled loudly, making Nicolas chuckle.

"Well if it's that urgent, I have a better idea. How about pizza? I know a place that should get it to us within 25 minutes."

*A BLT as a starter, a spanking, getting licked and fucked as a main dish, and pizza for dessert? Can life get any better than this?*

"Hell yeah!" she laughed.

Nicolas leaned over to grab his phone from the side table of the bed.

"That's it. Ordered!" he confirmed a few seconds later.

"Wow, that was fast. I just hope it doesn't have cubed avocado as a topping." Kimberly wrinkled her nose.

"Kimberly Jones, you're lucky I'm feeling a little tired right now, otherwise I would take you right back over my knee!"

Nicolas's voice wasn't truly serious and Kimberly giggled at his threat, pulling herself closer against the warmth of Nicolas's chest. She wondered if he loved her company as much as she loved his.

"What are you thinking of?" he asked.

Kimberly smiled.

"I was just wondering what I've enjoyed the most. When you spanked me, when you fingered me, when you licked me, or when you fucked me."

"Uff-. Well-. That's a difficult one. I don't even know what I liked best." He hugged her, looking down into her eyes. "I guess there's only one way to find out."

She giggled again, already guessing what he might be suggesting.

"Oh really, and what would that be?"

His hands moved down from her back to grab her ass as he pulled her on top of him.

"Next weekend, when I'm back, I will simply have

to spank you, finger you, lick you and fuck you again. And I am willing to repeat this every day of every weekend until you can make up your mind about what you like the most."

Kimberly's pussy responded to Nicolas's generous offer, wildly throbbing.

"But you are aware that it could take many, many, many weekends until I make up my mind?" she asked.

He planted a soft kiss on her lips.

"That is exactly what I am hoping for!"

"Have you been wearing it?" he asked.

"All week."

"And you're wearing it right now?"

"Just as you've told me to."

She was grinning, as she spoke into her cell phone, pretending it was regular small talk. In fact it was. It was the kind of dirty small talk that was absolutely normal between Nicolas and her.

"You really know how to get me hard Kimberly."

She laughed, imagining him sitting in the car, driving for two hours with a hard-on.

"I'm sorry Nic, but I really need to get back to work now. There's a bunch of hot guys in suits waiting for me to set up the coffee buffet."

"Watch out, you know what happened to your

backside last time you tried to make me jealous with the crowds of men that drool over you each day."

Not only was she excited for the long weekend with Nicolas, which was a mere three hours away, but she was also excited about what they'd planned to do that evening.

Excited and scared.

Maybe scared wasn't the right word, because she knew exactly that Nicolas wouldn't do anything to her that she didn't like.

Respect would probably describe it more closely.

Yes. She had a healthy amount of respect because fitting Nicholas's large member inside her tight hole sounded and felt amazing in all her fantasies but she wasn't so sure about actually doing it.

Kimberly pulled the large black tablecloth on the long banquet table. It reached all the way to the floor, to hide the legs of the table. She was skilled at tucking in the corners to make it look perfect.

Every step she took, every move she made, the heavy steel plug moved around inside of her, reminding her of the plans with Nicolas later on.

Almost a year had passed since she hit Nicolas with her soccer ball on the beach. They'd spend every single weekend together and most holidays.

She smiled, thinking of Nick, as she set up the coffee machine. This man was quite something.

Charming, irresistible, and persistent.

Mostly persistent.

Especially when it came to backdoor shenanigans. And as he wouldn't take no for an answer, Kimberly changed her tactic and told him, she wouldn't give him full access until he'd put a ring on her finger.

She absolutely loved it when he stroked across her most private area and played around there. Every time he did, she shut off her brain and indulged in the forbidden yet amazing sensations.

Who would have thought that oral sex with a finger in her pussy and another one stretching her tight ass out would make her climax more times in a row than anything else?

And then last week he did it. He went down on one knee with a box in his hands.

She was laughing, thinking it was all a big joke because the box was way too big for an engagement ring.

"Kimberly, you're the most intelligent, funniest, and sexiest woman I know. I want you to be mine, all of you. And forever. Will you marry me?"

Kimberly had stopped laughing immediately but then Nicolas opened the box and confused her even more.

He stayed so serious during his proposal, she still didn't understand how he did that.

He took out the stainless steel plug, grabbed her hand, and slipped the plug's ring on her finger. Then he closed her hand around the cold and heavy plug.

While it was probably the most original engagement ring and dirtiest proposal ever, the only thing that was annoying, was that she couldn't really tell anyone about it. But it also made it more special. It was their secret.

A romantic and dirty little secret.

It wasn't exactly the ring that she had imagined but she'd never been the jewellery-wearing type of woman anyhow, so it didn't matter.

---

"Please," she said again.

"Please, what?" he asked.

Kimberly moaned frustrated into the pillow. Nicolas had been gently spanking, fingering her, and tugging on the butt plug for almost an hour. He loved making her edge and so did she but enough was enough. Her cunt was needy and needed more.

"Please Nicolas, let me come!"

"Are you ready to come with my cock in your ass?"

*Am I?* she wondered.

Could she ever be ready for it?

But she wanted it. She wanted to fulfill all of her future husband's needs, just like he gave her everything she'd ever dreamed of.

"Yes," she answered.

She'd made the decision a long time ago, there was no chickening out now.

Kimberly felt her booty hole get stretched out again, but this time Nicolas didn't stop until the plug slipped completely out of her. It was a weird sensation making her pussy throb.

He helped her off his lap.

"Lie down on your back and spread your legs for me," Nicolas instructed.

Kimberly relaxed on the bed and enjoyed the life show of him generously covering his hard cock with lube. When Nicolas caught her staring, he smiled.

"Watch closely Kim. Every inch of it will soon be deep inside your beautiful ass."

His dick twitched in his hand, in agreement.

Kim's mouth felt dry and her heart was racing in her chest but it was a good type of nervousness, similar to the excitement that you get before going on stage.

Then Nicolas leaned forward and got on top of her, guiding his cock between her legs.

"Wrong hole my love," Kimberly giggled. Her pussy was so wet, that he accidentally slid inside of her.

She wrapped her hand around his thick dick to help him find the right entrance. Rubbing the tip of his cock against her bootyhole felt strange. She still wasn't sure how to fit all of him inside of her.

"Kiss me," Nicolas whispered, lowering his lips to hers.

He kissed her slowly.

While she held his dick against her entrance, Nicolas pushed gently against it.

She was surprised when she felt her booty hole opening up suddenly.

"Slowly," she called out.

Nicolas halted immediately, giving Kimberly time to adjust to his girth.

She let go of holding his cock and held onto his arms instead. She could feel herself stretching out but it didn't hurt. It was just like before, with the plug pushing in completely.

Relieved, she lifted her hips a little bit, pushing against Nicolas's dick, allowing him to dig deeper.

"Fuck, you're so so tight," Nicolas growled in her ear.

The twitching of his cock inside her ass felt ten times as intense as it did in her pussy. She knew that it was probably costing him a lot of self-discipline to not push inside of her.

Bit by bit, she let Nicolas go deeper and deeper until she finally felt his balls against her.

He was now all the way in and the feeling was so wrong and yet it felt so right.

The blood in her pussy pulsated, even though Nicolas wasn't even moving at all. Just being filled out by him like this was pure bliss.

"This is so dirty," she moaned, tilting her hips to feel him even deeper.

"And you love it, don't you?" he asked and started moving slowly.

Kimberly's eyes opened wide at the new sensation of his cock sliding out and back inside of her.

*Wow, just fucking wow*, she thought.

"Everything!" she moaned. "I love everything you do to me!"

"Good. I'll remind you of that the next time you're getting punished with the bath brush."

Kimberly's pussy throbbed as her ass was getting slow-fucked by Nicolas. With her legs wrapped around his hips, she let go, giving in to the fireworks of sensations that spread through her body.

The muscles in her ass squeezed Nicolas's cock as the powerful orgasm rolled through Kimberly.

Her deep moans filled the room, while Nicolas continued pushing in and out of her slowly, extending her orgasm.

---

"So?" Nicolas turned his head and kissed her on the forehead.

They were lying on the bed with Kimberly cradled in his arms.

She smiled. She felt shy talking about the dirty things they'd done just moments ago.

"It was okay, I guess," she answered.

"Okay?" Nicolas repeated.

She could hear the disappointment in his voice and burst out laughing.

"I feel embarrassed talking about it," she admitted.

"Aaah, I see," and then he whispered in her ear.

"But you weren't shy to take my cock all the way in your delicious butt."

Kimberly turned red and pushed herself up to escape Nicolas's arms but he hugged her even tighter.

"I'm not letting you go until you give me your honest feedback, beyond *okay*."

She loved that about Nicolas. He forced her to talk about her feelings, to talk about her desires and fears and he didn't take no for an answer just like that.

She covered her eyes with one hand, it was easier to say things in the dark sometimes.

"It was-. It felt-. So dirty. And it was scary but I think it was exactly that, that was so crazy hot about it. Just knowing, you know-, where your cock was? It's so wrong Nicolas, but it felt so right and wow-. The orgasm was so different, I felt it so deep in me, it was just crazy."

Nicolas tightened his hug.

She couldn't tell where he hid it, but the last thing she'd expected at that moment was him pulling out the small box, taking the ring out of it, and slipping it on her finger.

It was the perfect fit. She stared at her finger and her eyes went teary.

"You're mine now, Kimberly. All of you. Mine!"

The Strict Roommate

**"If you ever call me a baby again, I will take you over my knee. My hand is not broken."**

Olivia McKenzie is a passionate nurse, ready to move cities for her dream job in the Neonatal Intensive Care Unit. Limited to a handful of rooms she can afford, she decides to ignore all the red flags and move in with Jack.

Jack Hunter is the opposite of Olivia. He is the definition

of perfection and discipline, working out seven days a week and keeping his apartment spotless.

Olivia's messiness quickly turns into the main source of conflict between the two, causing a tense atmosphere. Her plan to stay out of Jack's life is thrown overboard when he breaks his foot.

Knowing that the accident was her fault, Olivia decides to take care of her grumpy roommate to relieve her guilt. It doesn't take long until sparks are flying and Jack's tough shell starts to crumble.

But when Olivia screws up again, she realizes that she'll never be good enough for Mr. Perfect…

*The Strict Roommate*** is a stand-alone of the Romantically Disciplined Series.

***This book contains graphic love scenes and consensual spankings.*

**"Lift your skirt and get over my knee."**

Mia Woods is the typical girl next door. She has great taste in music, is a hard worker and absolutely loves her new rental apartment which is just a short commute to her customer service job.

When her ultra-hot neighbor Dr. Jonathan Carter shows up at her door, Mia is ready to date him. But he's not coming to ask her out. It's quite the opposite. He wants to kick her out, and he's not making a secret out of it.

The eviction notice delivered by certified mail is a shock. Mia is desperate to do anything to make her landlord change his mind, however putting her backside's faith in his hands, is not at all what she expects. And even less, getting disciplined by two men.

Can the landlord's disciplinary actions improve the tense situation between Mia and her hostile neighbor or is she already one foot out of the door?

*Disciplined By Her Neighbor* is a stand-alone of the Steamy Doctors Series.

**This book contains MFM, graphic love scenes, and intense spankings.*

**"Are you ready to get disciplined?"**

Elizabeth Moore is a hopeless romantic, a huge fan of lava cakes, and thinks that men should be the ones to ask a woman out.

Her life gets thrown upside down when HR transfers her to the neurology clinic to fill in for a medical secretary. As if that isn't bad enough, Elizabeth gets rejected after breaking her own rules and asking a man out on a date.

The atmosphere in the doctor's office couldn't be more tense when the man who rejected her turns out to be Elizabeth's new boss, Dr. Charles Edwards.

As she learns the ins and outs of her new job, Dr. Edwards seems mainly concerned about pointing out her mistakes. His suggestion to teach her the old-fashioned way sounds more than exciting but discipline isn't the only thing he's handing out.

When Dr. Edwards only has eyes for the keynote speaker of the Neurology Symposium, Elizabeth finds a way to get back at him.

Will Dr. Edwards choose a secretary over a doctor or has Elizabeth only been an office fling all along?

*Disciplined By Her Boss* ** is a stand-alone of the Steamy Doctors Series.

***This book contains graphic love scenes and consensual spankings.*

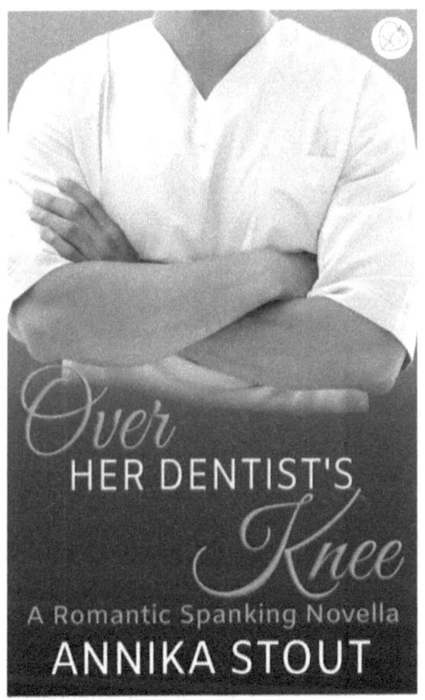

**I want you to trust me with your dirtiest fantasies, Victoria."**

Victoria Córdova is a tough police officer and passionate soccer player. She likes being in charge and nothing scares her. There's only one exception…dentists.

Dr. Arthur Crutchfield, her dental surgeon, is dreamman material. Victoria can't tell if the sparks between them are real or an illusion caused by the pain medication.

When she is confronted with her dentist on patrol, Victoria is torn between showing her tough side and submitting to the man who has the ability to make her heart speed up and calm down at the same time.

Arthur is fascinated by his patient's fierce identity. Nothing turns him on more than bending a strong woman over his knee and letting him take control of her pleasure.

He's sure about one thing though, friends with benefits is all he has to offer…

*Over Her Dentist's Knee* is a stand-alone of the Steamy Doctors Series.

**This book contains graphic love scenes and consensual spankings.*

Annika Stout's relationship is a real-life spanking romance. Whenever she's not writing, she is most probably bent over Mr. Stout's knee to find more inspiration.

It wasn't always like that, it took her years to be confident enough to say what she wants and needs. She hopes that her books can help others do the same.

Annika offers contemporary spanking romance without the dark BDSM stuff. Just your typical guy next door, a hot boss or co-worker who isn't afraid to make a strong woman's fantasy come true.

Why not give one of Annika's books to your partner to introduce him/her to your kink? You can read it together or leave a note with it.

If you feel weird about it, just remember that spankos are considered vanillas within the BDSM community.